Chapter One: "The Missing Mascot"

Written by Giulie Speziani

Artwork, Lettering and Pinup by Penny Candy Studios

DANVILLE
DANVILLE JUNIOR HIGH
9 PM
munch munch
DANVILLE SAINTS
DANVILLE SAINTS
FWIP
DANVILLE SAINTS

MISTY WAS FINE LAST NIGHT, SIR. I DIDN'T NOTICE ANYTHING STRANGE.
DID THEY LEAVE A RANSOM NOTE, PERHAPS?
WHO'S THEY?
SIGH
THE CRIMINALS.
OH NO. NO NOTES FROM ANYONE, PRINCIPAL MCCARTHY.
LET'S BE SURE THEY DIDN'T STEAL ANYTHING ELSE.
HOW CAN YOU TELL IT'S A THEY AND NOT AN IT? IT COULD HAVE BEEN A COYOTE...
...OR BIGFOOT.
I'LL JUST BE IN MY OFFICE.
MASON MIDDLE SCHOOL 7TH PERIOD MATH CLASS
Example 1:
hmm
DALLAS CASH
INVESTIGATOR & TENACIOUS TECHIE
WHO SWIPED THE SAINTS' MASCOT?
NOTES
DANVILLE VOICE
GONE!

DING
DING
DING
DID YOU GET THE SCOOP ON THE GOAT?
YEAH. I SENT YOU THE LIST OF ALL THE GAMES THE DANVILLE SAINTS ARE PLAYING THIS SEASON.
I DON'T THINK IT'S A RIVAL SCHOOL, CARRIE.
HERE WE GO AGAAAAIN.
CASH, LET'S RULE OUT THE OBVIOUS FIRST, THEN GO DEEPER. THE ANSWER COULD BE STARING US IN THE FACE.
INEZ CARRIE, INVESTIGATOR & CAPTAIN OF THE WRESTLING TEAM
OR HIDING BEHIND YOU
!!
TADA!
LET'S REVIEW THE VIDEO FROM LAST NIGHT & SEE IF IT RECORDED THE GOAT SNATCHER.
THE TIMECODE SKIPS AHEAD FROM 9:11 PM TO 9:13 PM.
A GLITCH?
THIS FOOTAGE HAS BEEN ALTERED.
IF SOMEONE DID FIX THE VIDEO, WHO DID & WHY?
THERE'S ONLY ONE WAY TO FIND OUT.

MASON MIDDLE
ENTRANCE
DANVILLE MIDDLE SCHOOL
YOU HAVE CLEARANCE, RIGHT?
OF COURSE!
STUDENT IDENTIFICATION
DANVILLE STUDENT
CASH, DALLAS
STUDENT IDENTIFICATION
DANVILLE STUDENT
PUSH
EASY-CHEESY.

TJ WONG, EDITOR OF THE DANVILLE VOICE, PIZZA ENTHUSIAST
I'VE BARELY UPLOADED THE "MISSING MISTY" STORY AND ALREADY YOU TWO SHOW UP.
WE WASTE NO TIME, TJ.
HAS PRINCIPAL MCCARTHY TALKED TO THE FUZZ YET?
HE'S FILING A REPORT WITH THEM AS WE SPEAK.
HE COULD BE A SUSPECT, TOO.
DOUBTFUL. MCCARTHY WAS AT AN ALUMNI EVENT ON THE OTHER SIDE OF TOWN. AND IF THIS WAS A PRANK, THERE'D BE PHOTOS POSTED ON THE INTERNET BY NOW, BUT NONE HAVE SURFACED.
BRAGGY PRANKSTERS ARE EASY TO SPOT.
HOW ABOUT ANY RIVAL SCHOOLS? THOSE SHOULDER PAD SMASHERS ARE ALWAYS PICKING ON EACH OTHER.
THAT'S A NEGATIVE.
WE'RE WINLESS THIS SEASON, SO THERE'S NO REAL REASON --

HEY TJ!
WHO ARE THESE GOOBERS?
I'VE NEVER SEEN THEM IN ANY OF MY CLASSES.
YEAH! THIS IS SAINTS-ONLY TERRITORY.
MY FRIENDS ARE COOL, BRIAN. YOU, RYAN, AND IAN CAN BE EASY.
WE'RE JUST ON OUR WAY OUT.
YOUR BEST BET IS TO RUN OUT OF HERE.
WE DON'T RUN.
GLIDING IS MORE OUR SPEED.
SNIK!
POP!
GOOD LUCK, GUYS!
LATER, TJ!

YOU LIGHTWEIGHTS BETTER STAY OFF OUR TURF!
20
GLAD WE'RE MAKING FRIENDS.
FORGET THE HELMET HEADS.
WE GOTTA SEARCH MISTY'S CAGE FOR CLUES.
THE FENCE IS STILL INTACT AND LOCKED. THEY MUST'VE PICKED MISTY OFF THE GROUND WITH THEIR BARE HANDS.
NO PRETEEN CAN PICK UP A 50 POUND GOAT WITHOUT DUSTING UP SOME DIRT. ACCORDING TO MY SPYTECHZ APP, THIS GRASS IS FOOT-PRINT FREE.
SPY TECHZ
MAYBE THEY ASKED THEIR BIG BROTHER OR BIG SISTER FOR HELP.
OR MAYBE A *FRATERNITY* BROTHER.
ALPHA DELTA DELTA.

THE CASH HOUSEHOLD, 7:54PM
friendFace
PROFILE
TEDWALLINGER
19, M
ALPHA DELTA DELTA
PRIME SUSPECT, TED WALLINGER. HE IS PART OF THE ALPHA DELTA DELTA FRAT AND OVERALL KNOWN PRANKSTER.
AND OLDER BROTHER OF TAB WALLINGER, A DANVILLE STUDENT.
NO TPS OR NES OR WHATEVER YOU'RE PLAY-ING NOW, MR. DALLAS CASH. DID YOU FINISH YOUR HOMEWORK YET?
YES, AND CARRIE FINISHED HERS AS WELL.
THANKS MOM!
THANKS MRS. CASH!
OH GOOD. PIZZA BITES ARE IN THE OVEN.
CALLING SUSPECT NUMBER ONE.
CALLING...
HOPE HE'S HOME.

WHAT DO YOU WANT?
YOU'VE GOT TWO MINUTES BEFORE VAMPIRE DIARIES COMES BACK ON.
WHERE WAS YOUR BROTHER, TED, LAST NIGHT? DID HE DRIVE ANYWHERE, VISIT ANY FRIENDS?
NAH. HE WAS TOO BUSY DOING HIS BENCH PRESSES.
WITH A GOAT, PERHAPS?
NAH.
HE WAS IN STRENGTH TRAINING WITH ME. AS IN -- HE BENCH PRESSES ME. HE GIVES ME A CANDY BAR EVERY TIME I HELP OUT.
THE MORE FAT I GAIN, THE MORE MUSCLE HE GAINS. WIN WIN.
INTERESTING.
WELL, THANKS FOR YOUR INPUT.
PEACE OUT, SPY DORKS.
hup!
huff
puff
huff
tada!

WELL THAT RULES HIM OUT.
MAYBE MORE CLUES WILL SURFACE TOMORROW.
KNOCK KNOCK
ARE WE EXPECTING COMPANY, MOM? THERE'S NOT ENOUGH PIZZA ROLLS FOR EVERYBODY.
NO, DALLAS. IT'S PROBABLY JUST THE POSTAL SERVICE LEAVING A PACKAGE FOR ME.
AT THIS HOUR?
KNOCK KNOCK
WE GOT IT, MRS. CASH.

IT'S NOT ALPHA DELTA DELTA!
?!
I'M NOT SCARED.
IF THAT TRANSLATES TO "I'M FREAKED OUT," THEN YES, I AGREE.
IT'S NOT ALPHA DELTA DELTA!

GOOD MORNING, STUDENTS. THIS IS VICE PRINCIPAL TANAKA SPEAKING. I'M GLAD TO REPORT THAT OUR SISTER SCHOOL DANVILLE JUNIOR HIGH HAVE HAD THEIR MASCOT MISTY THE GOAT RETURNED TO THEM.
AND OUR LUNCH SPECIAL TODAY IS ALMOND-CRUSTED TILAPIA WITH RICE PILAF.
LEARNING
BOO!
NOT AGAIN!
AW!
WELL I GUESS THIS CASE IS CLOSED. MAYBE THE OTHER FRAT BOYS GOT COLD FEET AND RETURNED MISTY BEFORE ANYONE FOUND THEM OUT.
HMM. NOT CONVINCED.
I KNEW YOU WERE GOING TO SAY THAT.
THIS LOOKS LIKE THE SAME GOAT THAT WAS STOLEN.
SAME BREED, HEIGHT, HORNS, AND EVEN HAS HIS SCHOOL CAPE ON.
DANVILLE SAINTS
YEAH... LET'S GO.
WEIRD THAT THE SCHOOLS'S TOP NOTCH SURVEILLANCE DIDN'T RECORD ANYTHING. SPECIFICALLY DURING THE TIMES WHEN MISTY WAS STOLEN, THEN RETURNED.
YET NO TRACE OF ***WHO*** HACKED THE SYSTEM.
SCIEN
NOT HACKED, BUT MAYBE HEXED...
BAHH
UNTIL NEXT TIME...!

Pinup by Jay Reed

Chapter Two:
"We Interrupt This Program"
Written by Giulie Speziani
Artwork and Lettering by
Penny Candy Studios
Pinup by Christina "Steenz" Stewart

www.bloobtubetv.com
WE INTERRUPT THIS PROGRAM
WRITER: GIULIE SPEZIANI ARTIST: PENNY CANDY STUDIOS
GOOD AFTERNOON, I'M JACKIE KIRBEE AND THIS IS THE GRAPEVINE.
RECENT RIVALRY BETWEEN FOOD TRUCKS, MR. SLUSHY AND MS. SNOW CONE HAVE REACHED NEW HEIGHTS.
BOTH TRY TO CORNER THE MARKET BY APPEALING TO KIDS AND PARENTS ALIKE BUT THIS PAST SUNDAY PROVED TO BE DIFFICULT.
IT GOT SO HOT OUT, THEY HAD TO CHANGE THEIR MENU TO SELL NATURALLY MELTED SHAVED ICE.
ALSO KNOWN AS SUGAR WATER.
IT'S THE LAST WEEK OF SCHOOL AND HERE NOW TO GIVE US A FEW TIPS ON HOW TO ENJOY THE SUMMER BREAK, OUR FAVORITE TWINS, JERRY & JOE.
HOW ARE YA, GUYS?

JOE AND I ARE DOING WELL, JACKIE!
WE CAN'T WAIT TO TELL YOU THE BEST TIPS FOR YOUR AWESOME POOL PARTY.
LET'S GO, JERRY!
TIP #1
CANNON BALL!!
DON'T PUT THE FOOD TABLE NEAR THE POOL.
NOBODY LIKES SOGGY CHIPS.
TIP #2
NO RUNNING !!
DON'T CHALLENGE A MEMBER OF THE SWIM TEAM TO A RELAY RACE.
CHANCES ARE, YOU'LL LOSE.

SAVE FACE AND OPT OUT.
MARCO?
PLAY MARCO POLO INSTEAD!
DO STOCK UP ON AQUATIC TOYS LIKE BEACH BALLS, FOAM NOODLES, AND A VOLLYBALL NET.
TIP #3
OR IF YOU'RE ON A BUDGET, WATER BALLOONS ARE THE WAY TO GO.
AND FINALLY, DO STAY SAFE.
AND HAVE FUN!
BACK TO YOU, JACKIE!

THANKS GUYS. AND NOW WE'LL SHIFT GEARS TO UPDATE YOU ON THE LATEST OF THE LANGFORD SCHOOL GYM FIRE.
LAST WEEK WE REPORTED THAT THERE WERE NO SUSPECTS.
UNTIL NOW.
BEATRICE BELL, A RETIRED SCHOOL TEACHER, DENIES BURNING DOWN LANGFORD GYM DESPITE AUTHORITIES HAVING FOUND EVIDENCE OF BOLT CUTTERS AND AN EMPTY FUEL CAN IN HER CAR.
I DON'T THINK SHE DID IT.
LOOKS LIKE WE GOT WORK TO DO.
SCHOOL'S ENDING BUT OUR JOB IS JUST BEGINNING!

CASH CARRIE
CONCEPT ART
Very early Carrie
Wrestling Team
TAP
TAP TAP
TAP
TAP
Early Cash
mode indicator light
Tech Glasses

Chapter Three: "Saturday Detention"

Written by Giulie Speziani
Artwork, Lettering and Pinup by Marcus Kwame Anderson

THE DANVILLE VOICE

50 Cents

The Goat Napper Is Still At Large

By Tina Williams

DANVILLE — Weary students and faculty breathed a collective sigh of relief last week when beloved mascot, Misty the Goat reappeared in her pen. Danville police chief Jackson Jackson Jr. said, "This town has been through enough recently. The last thing we need is folks pointing fingers. We all love Misty, and frankly, we are all Misty."

Jackson was responding to accusations that the Danville P.D. had not been proactive enough in naming suspects in the goat napping. "I assure you, we are working around the clock to bring this monster to justice. We're pursuing several leads at this time."

Reactions to the case of the missing goat have been varied

MRS. BELL?
IT'S US, DALLAS CASH AND INEZ CARRIE.
MMHM... STERLING...
KIDS! *COUGH* SORRY, I WAS IN THE MIDDLE OF A DREAM.
NO NEED TO APOLOGIZE.
AT LEAST THE TOWN FOUND IT MORE FITTING TO HAVE YOU UNDER HOUSE ARREST GIVEN YOUR CONDITION, MRS. BELL.
THAT RETRO GPS ANKLE BRACELET SURE LOOKS COOL.
IT'S ITCHY!
BUT YOU CAN HAVE VISITORS!
WITH MASON MIDDLE'S MOST PRESTIGIOUS DETECTIVES, YES, THERE'S THAT.
SCHOOL'S BACK IN SESSION AND WE'VE BEEN HEARING SOME STRANGE THINGS HAPPENING OVER AT LANGFORD.
STRANGE THINGS HAVE BEEN HAPPENING THERE FOR A LONG TIME. EVER SINCE PRINCIPAL STERLING TOOK OVER.

WE'VE BEEN TRYING TO SEE THE CONNECTION BETWEEN THE GYM FIRE AND STEPFORD — *I MEAN* LANGFORD'S STRANGE STUDENTS.
YOU WANT TO KNOW *WHY* I BURNED DOWN THAT GYM?
I SAW.... *VOODOO.*
"ONE SATURDAY MORNING..."
HERE CHOTCHKIE, CHOTCHKIE. WHERE'S MY PRETTY KITTY?
"I HEARD SOME CHANTING."
OOH, AHH AHH. VEDA VEDA DERP DERP.
"I TRIED TO SEE WHAT WAS GOING ON IN THERE."

"I SAW ONE OF MY FAVORITE STUDENTS, NOAH. I WAS HIS ART TEACHER IN THIRD GRADE. HE'S IN SIXTH GRADE NOW AND LOOKS TO HAVE CHANGED OVER NIGHT."
MRS. BELL, EVERYONE GOES THROUGH *THAT* CHANGE.
NOT LIKE THIS.
HE'S UNDER A VOODOO SPELL. JUST LIKE *DANVILLE'S MASCOT*, MISTY.
WHY DIDN'T YOU CALL THE POLICE?
I FELL ASLEEP.
WELCOME
WHERE DO WE FIT IN?
LANGFORD IS TRYING TO IMPROVE THEIR SCHOOL PERFORMANCE SCORE BY BRAINWASHING KIDS TO ACE THEIR EXAMS. BUT THEIR UNIQUE PERSONALITIES ARE NOW *GONE*.
NOW THAT THE GYM BURNED DOWN, SATURDAY DETENTIONS NEED TO FIND ANOTHER SPOT. *YOU TWO* HAVE TO FIGURE THAT OUT. AND *SOON!*
AND ANOTHER THING. AND THIS IS IMPORTANT--

ZZZZZZ.
GUESS IT WASN'T THAT IMPORTANT.
AND MORE IMPORTANTLY, WHO'S THE NEXT VICTIM?
TIME TO PUT ON A UNIFORM, SNEAK INTO LANGFORD AND FIND OUT WHERE THE NEXT DETENTION WILL BE.

BEFORE WE BARGE IN THAT STRANGE SCHOOL, LET'S REVIEW THESE STUDENTS WHO'VE RECEIVED SATURDAY DETENTION. ALL TWELVE OF THEM.
DETENTION
Student: Noah W.
Saturday, 9:00 am
Reason for Detention:
FOOD FIGHT
THERE'S NOAH. THE REASON FOR DETENTION...
FOOD FIGHT?
YEAH THAT'S WHAT THEY SAY. BUT NOAH WAS AN ARTIST NOT A FIGHTER. HE WAS JUST USING FOOD AS FINGER PAINT.
WAS?
EVER SINCE THAT SATURDAY DETENTION, HE'S DIFFERENT. A TOTAL CYBORG NOW. THAT'S WHY WE DON'T HANG OUT ANYMORE.
THE ONLY WAY TO CONFIRM MRS. BELL'S STORY IS TO TALK TO NOAH HIMSELF.
IF HE'S GAME.
DON'T WORRY, KWAN. WE CAN COAX HIM OUT OF HIS SHELL.
SKRRRRITCH
I HOPE YOU DO. I MISS MY BEST FRIEND.
SINCE THE GYM BURNED DOWN, WHERE DO YOU HAVE P.E.?
OUTSIDE ON THE FIELD.

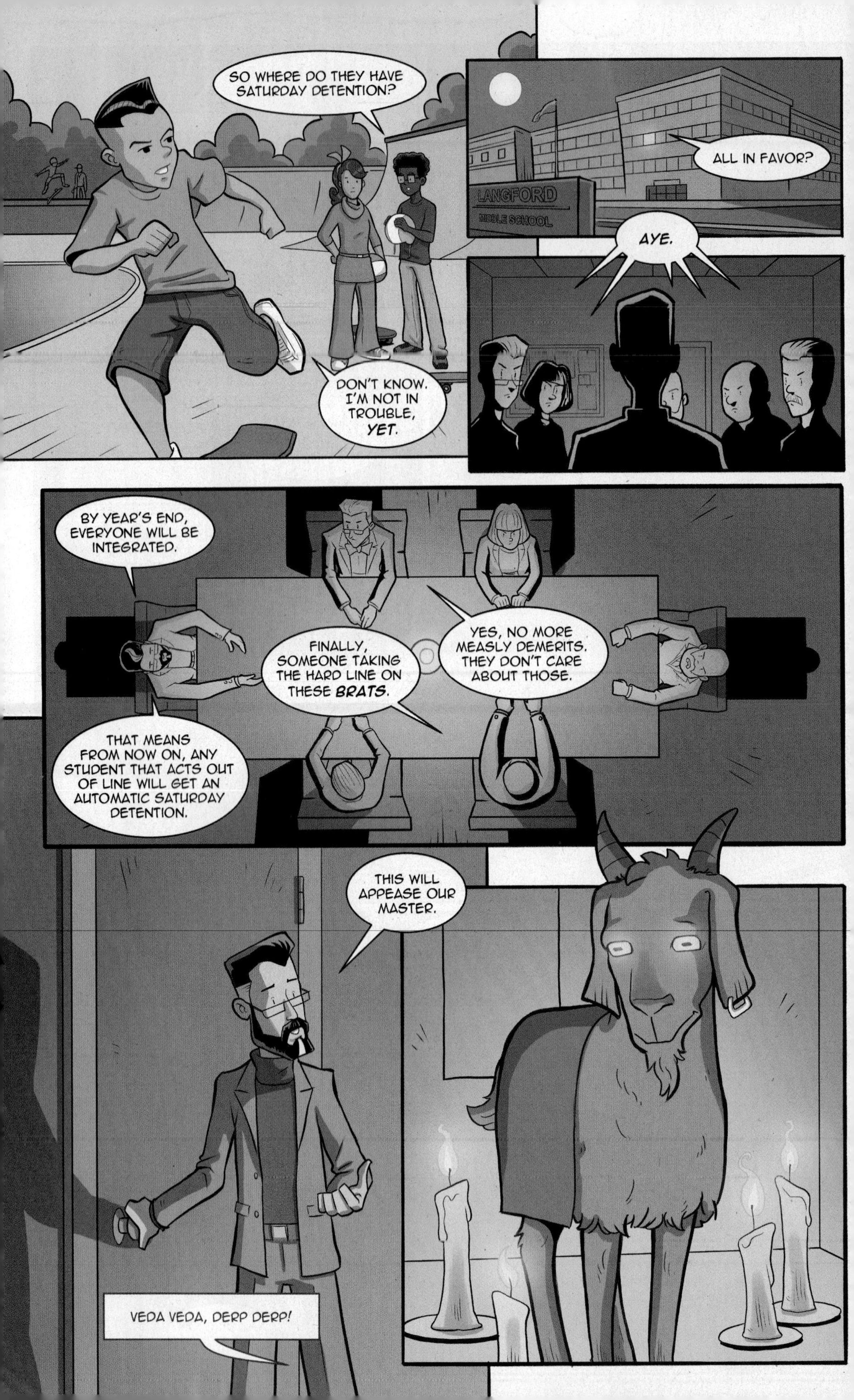
SO WHERE DO THEY HAVE SATURDAY DETENTION?
DON'T KNOW. I'M NOT IN TROUBLE, YET.
LANGFORD
MIDDLE SCHOOL
ALL IN FAVOR?
AYE.
BY YEAR'S END, EVERYONE WILL BE INTEGRATED.
THAT MEANS FROM NOW ON, ANY STUDENT THAT ACTS OUT OF LINE WILL GET AN AUTOMATIC SATURDAY DETENTION.
FINALLY, SOMEONE TAKING THE HARD LINE ON THESE BRATS.
YES, NO MORE MEASLY DEMERITS. THEY DON'T CARE ABOUT THOSE.
THIS WILL APPEASE OUR MASTER.
VEDA VEDA, DERP DERP!

LANGFORD
WE STRIVE FOR PERFECTION, NO MATTER WHAT.
WE DON'T HAVE MUCH TIME, LET'S TALK TO NOAH AND GET OUT OF HERE.
ACCORDING TO HIS ONLINE CLASS SCHEDULE, HE'S IN STUDY HALL.
PSST. HEY NOAH.
I'M STUDYING.
WE JUST WANT TO KNOW, WHAT HAPPENED WHEN YOU WENT TO SATURDAY DETENTION.
I IMPROVED.
WHOA. WAIT. NOAH.
WHAT ARE YOU LOOKING FOR?
ANSWERS. WHERE DO THEY HOLD SATURDAY DETENTIONS NOW?
ON THE THIRD FLOOR. TAKE THE STAIRS.

C'MON CASH.
I'M RIGHT BEHIND YOU.
WE'RE ALMOST THERE. KEEP UP!
I AM!
THIS WAY!
NEXT TIME... *HUFF* WE'RE TAKING... *HUFF* THE ELEVATOR.
NOW WE'LL GET SOME--

--ANSWERS!
OH. NICE VIEW.
NOT FUNNY. I CAN'T BELIEVE WE FELL FOR IT.
OLDEST JOKE IN THE BOOK.
THEY'RE NOT GETTING AWAY THAT EASY.
THERE HAS TO BE A WAY TO FIND OUT WHERE THE NEXT BRAINWASHING CEREMONY TAKES PLACE.
WHAT ARE YOU *PLANNING* TO DO?

BOOM!
NOW THAT I HAVE YOUR ATTENTION--
WE WANT WOOD SHOP CLASS! WE WANT HOME EC! WE WANT UNDERWATER BASKET WEAVING!
EXIT
WHO ARE YOU? GET BACK HERE!
SOMEONE'S MAD.
Periodic Table of Elements
IS THIS WHAT WE WANT?
NO!
THEN JOIN ME! WE DON'T NEED THEM. LET'S WALK OUT!

OH NO YOU DON'T.
AUTOMATIC DETENTION!
YOU TAKE THIS DOWN TO THE PRINCIPAL'S OFFICE, RIGHT NOW, YOUNG MAN.
Detention Slip
Date:
Reason: Disobedience
signature:
UH-OH. I GUESS I'M IN TROUBLE.
EVERYONE CLEAN UP YOUR STATIONS NOW UNLESS YOU WANT A POP QUIZ.
AW.
AW.
AW.

I SEE THAT YOU'VE RECENTLY TRANSFERRED. WHAT A SHAME YOU HAVEN'T ADAPTED TO OUR ENVIRONMENT.
PRINCIPAL STERLING
DETENTION
Disobedience
DO I HAVE TO WRITE AN ESSAY FOR PUNISHMENT?
NO, AN ESSAY WON'T WORK. HOW 'BOUT YOU COME IN FOR SATURDAY DETENTION? AT THE BANQUET HALL ACROSS THE STREET. 8 AM SHARP. WE'LL HELP YOU ADAPT.
I'LL BE THERE.
I CAN'T BELIEVE YOU DID THAT. WHAT IF YOU BECOME ONE OF THEM?
I WON'T BE CONVERTED. I'M TOO SMART.
THEY'LL BRAINWASH YOU.
THE ONLY WAY WE REALLY KNOW WHAT HAPPENS IN DETENTION IS TO EXPERIENCE IT FIRST HAND.
I CAN'T WATCH YOU BE A GUINEA PIG.
I KNOW WHAT I'M DOING.
SO DO I.

ZZZZZ
MRS. BELL. MRS. BELL, WAKE UP.
MMM.. COOKIES... MRHMRM.
TOOT
SORRY, MRS. B. BUT I NEED TO TALK TO YOU.
WHERE'S YOUR PARTNER IN CRIME?
HE'S IN OVER HIS HEAD.
WHAT WAS THAT IMPORTANT THING YOU WERE GOING TO MENTION? BEFORE YOU DOZED OFF.
OH! NOAH SAT ON A CHAIR INSIDE A PAINTED CIRCLE. ONCE HE SAT DOWN, THE CEREMONY ENDED. HE WAS CURSED.
WHATEVER DALLAS DOES, MAKE SURE HE DOESN'T SIT IN THAT CHAIR.

SATURDAY, 7:45 AM
HI MRS. CASH, IS DALLAS AROUND? HE HASN'T ANSWERED MY TEXTS.
SORRY CARRIE, BUT HE WENT OVER HIS DATA PLAN AND I TOOK AWAY HIS PHONE. HE LEFT A WHILE AGO TO GET HIS MOPED TUNED-UP.
OH, I SEE. NEVER MIND. I'LL CATCH UP WITH HIM LATER.
HMMM.
THE ONLY THING THAT'S GOING TO BE *TUNED-UP* IS CASH'S BRAIN IF I DON'T SAVE HIM!

I HOPE I'M NOT TOO LATE.
C+C
WHOA!
SCREEEECH!
41
3
23
8
TODAY OF ALL DAYS!
CC1
BETTER TAKE A SHORT CUT.

DALLAS! THEY'LL PUT A CURSE ON YOU! STAY AWAY FROM THE CHAIR.
WHY DOESN'T HE HEAR ME?
SLAM!
BE CAREFUL.
SATURDAY, 8:01 AM.
YOU'RE LATE.
YUP.
AFTER TODAY YOU WON'T EVER BE.
DO I HAVE TO BALANCE BOOKS ON MY HANDS?
NO. BUT YOU HAVE TO REPEAT AFTER ME.
OH OH MA BI DA.

VEDA VEDA, DERP DERP.
I HAVE TO GET MRS. BELL.
ZZZZZ
SIT TIGHT MRS. B, WE'RE ALMOST THERE!
C+C
CC1

MRS BELL IS MAKING A BREAK FOR IT!
BELL
WEEOOOH WEEOOOH WEEOOOH
357
603
702
THEY SHOULD BE HERE ANY MINUTE.
THE CEREMONY IS COMPLETE.
WEEOOOH WEEOOOH
THERE THEY ARE!
UM... WE'RE REHEARSING A PLAY?
HA! NICE TRY.

I GOT IT ALL RIGHT HERE. THEY WERE TRYING TO CONTROL ME AGAINST MY WILL.
AND HOW DID THESE KIDS CHANGE BUT YOU DIDN'T?
WITH THIS.
•REC 45:36
I MADE THESE TINY NOISE-CANCELING EAR BUDS. I NODDED ALONG BUT COULDN'T HEAR ANYTHING. I TUNED THEM OUT.
AND FURTHER PROOF, THERE'S THIS CD OF HYPNOTIC CHANTS FOR YOUNG ADULTS.
WHAT'S THAT PRINCIPAL STERLING? I CAN'T HEAR YOU.
YOU HAVEN'T HEARD THE LAST OF ME, CASH AND CARRIE!
WHAT WILL HAPPEN TO THOSE LANGFORD STUDENTS?
NOW THAT THE PRINCIPAL IS GONE, OUTTA SIGHT OUTTA MIND. THE SPELL WILL WEAR OFF AND EVERYONE GOES BACK TO NORMAL INCLUDING NOAH.
AND MRS. BELL IS FREE... TO FALL ASLEEP OUTSIDE HER HOUSE, AGAIN.
WHAT'S NEXT?
SOUR GUMMIES AND A MATINEE.
GREAT IDEA!
FINALLY WE'RE ON THE SAME PAGE!
THE END.

CASH+CARRIE
1
Pinup by Justin Castaneda
2015

Chapter Four:

"Now You See Me"

Written by Giulie Speziani

Artwork by Andy Jewett

Lettering by Justin Birch

Pinup by Meg Daunting

I THINK WE'RE GOING AROUND IN CIRCLES.
YEAH THIS ALL LOOKS FAMILIAR. ROCK, ROCK AND MORE ROCK.
WHEREVER THERE'S A DRAFT, THAT'S WHERE WE SHOULD GO. IT'LL LEAD US OUT OF HERE.
PROBLEM IS, I DON'T FEEL ANY DRAFT.
AND WE'RE OUT OF RANGE SO MY GPS DOESN'T WORK.
GPS
OUT OF RANGE
....
SQUEEK!
SQUEEK!
WHAT'S THAT?
MOST PROBABLY BATS. THEY'RE HARMLESS TO US HUMANS. WHAT I FIND SCARY IS THAT WE'RE LOST.

LOOKS LIKE WE HAVE TWO OPTIONS.
OPTION NUMBER ONE CAN LEAD US FARTHER DOWN TO AN EVENTUAL DEAD END.
OR OPTION NUMBER TWO, CAN LEAD US OUT OR LOOP US BACK HERE.
WE HAVE TO MAKE A DECISION.
LET'S FLIP FOR IT. HEADS, OPTION ONE. TAILS, OPTION TWO.
GREAT. THERE GOES MY QUARTER.
CLICK
CLICK
I DON'T GET IT. THESE WERE FULLY CHARGED.

AH! I KNEW IT WAS GOING TO BE HEADS.
SO OPTION ONE.
ACK!
YOU SCARED US. ARE YOU LOST LIKE WE ARE?
HEY WAIT, WHERE YA GOING?
I THINK SHE WANTS US TO FOLLOW HER.
KINDA QUIET, AIN'T SHE?
BUT FRIENDLY!

WHEN WE GET BACK I HAVE TO DO THE DISHES. WE HAVE A DISH WASHING MACHINE BUT MY MOM STILL WANTS ME TO RINSE THE GUCK OUT.
MY WEEKEND CHORES INCLUDE TAKING OUT THE TRASH AND CLEANING OUT HAMLET'S CAGE.
I WONDER IF THERE'S ANY SPIDERS DOWN HERE.
THERE'S SPIDERS EVERYWHERE.
I THINK I FEEL A DRAFT.
ME TOO. MUST BE GETTING CLOSE.
GLAD THAT'S OVER.
WELL THANKS TO OUR GUIDE--
OH! WHERE SHE GO?
STRANGE INDEED.
LET'S GO BEFORE IT GETS DARK.
I KNOW THE WAY!

DAYS LATER...
ART
NOW CLASS, WE'RE ENTERING PHOTOGRAPHY IN THE EARLY TWENTIETH CENTURY.
AS YOU CAN SEE, THE PEOPLE IN THE PHOTOGRAPHS ARE NOT SMILING.
OF COURSE NOT, THEY HAD NO INTERNET!
AHEM. TO PROCESS A SINGLE PHOTOGRAPH IT REQUIRES A CHEMICAL SOLUTION BATH...
WHEN DO YOU THINK WE'LL SEE A REAL PICTURE OF BIGFOOT?
DON'T HOLD YOUR BREATH.
WE SHOULD TAKE A CLASS TRIP TO ROSWELL, NEW MEXICO.
LET ME GUESS... TO VISIT THE ALIEN MUSEUM.
IT'S EDUCATIONAL.

THIS PHOTOGRAPH WAS ACTUALLY TAKEN NEARBY BACK IN NINETEEN THIRTY-ONE.
THE GIRL YOU SEE HERE WENT MISSING. SHE WAS ABOUT YOUR AGE.
SHE LEFT HER HOME TO GO EXPLORING IN THE WOODS...

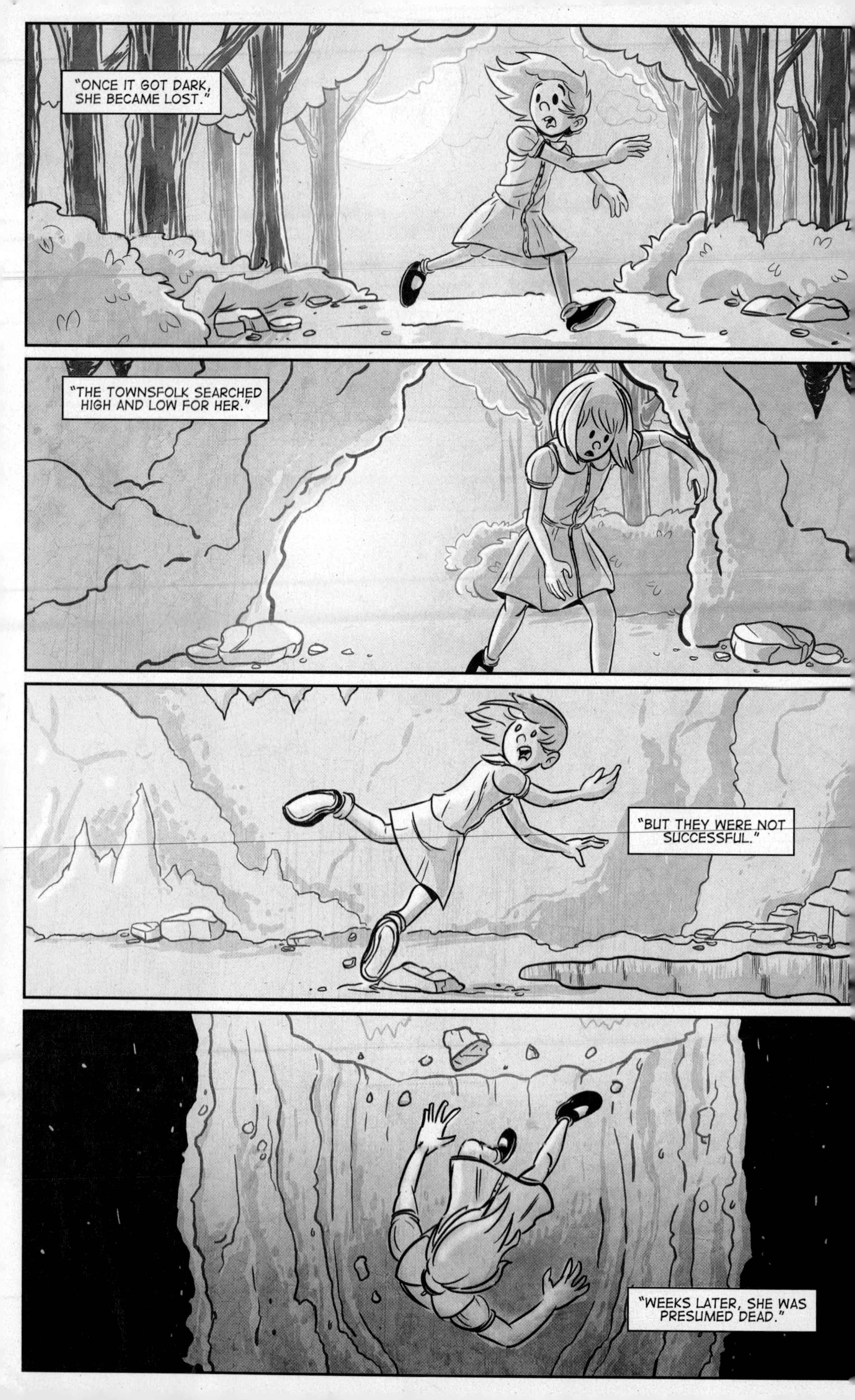
"ONCE IT GOT DARK, SHE BECAME LOST."
"THE TOWNSFOLK SEARCHED HIGH AND LOW FOR HER."
"BUT THEY WERE NOT SUCCESSFUL."
"WEEKS LATER, SHE WAS PRESUMED DEAD."

THIS WAY TO THE CAFETERIA!
DALLAS. DOESN'T SHE LOOK LIKE...
YES, INEZ. IT'S THE GIRL FROM THE CAVE.
BUT HOW?
SOME THINGS ARE BETTER LEFT UN-EXPLAINED.
OH THERE'S AN EXPLANATION ALL RIGHT. I JUST CAN'T BELIEVE IT. MAYBE SHE'S A RELATIVE?
NOPE. THEY DON'T LOOK SIMILAR; THEY'RE EXACTLY THE SAME PERSON.
WELL WHOEVER SHE WAS, SHE SAVED US.
THE END.

Pinup by Shauna J. Grant

Chapter Five:
"Fetch Quest"
Story Plot by Shawn Pryor
Story, Artwork, Lettering and
Pinup by
Chris Ludden and Ginger Dee

FOLDING CHAIR FRENZY!
AAAARRRAAAGH! AAIIEEE!
IT'S-A-ME
WAAAAA!
FETCH QUEST
I WIN AGAIN!
INTERNATIONAL DEBATORS 2
PLAYER 1 WINS!
THIS ISN'T LIKE A *REAL* DEBATE.
THERE'S NO REASONING. NO PERSUASION.
IT JUST MEASURES WHO YELLS THE LOUDEST.
WHICH I AM BEST AT!
OMIGOSH YOU'RE CASH AND CARRIE!

TRUE YOU FOUND OUT
WHAT WAS IN THE MEATLOAF
AND ALSO SAVED THE MATHBEE
COLONY IN SPRINGFIELD AND
TYRANNOSAURUS
SOCCER FIELD
APPLESAUCE
TRAIN DEPOT
THEIR BASKET
TEACHER
ISLAND
MOUSTACHES
GOAL OCTOPUS
...DESIGNED A WEBSITE FOR THE AV CLUB AND-
KID, PEOPLE SAY *A LOT* OF THINGS ABOUT US.
BELIEVE THE GOOD BITS!
YES! GREAT! YOU CAN HELP ME!
MY DOG'S MISSING! KIDNAPPED? *RUN OFF? KAPOOF!*
BACK UP A BIT.
TO THE PART WHERE YOU TELL US YOUR NAME.
MIKE!
MICHAEL!
OR MIKEY!
OR MIC!
OK, *MIKE.*
THE START OF ANY INVESTIGATION IS RETRACING YOUR STEPS!
WHERE'D YOU LAST SEE YOUR DOG?

SOON!
...AND SHE'S HUGE! LIKE A TANK! AND SHE'S GOT ONE EYE.
HUH! I'D REMEMBER A DOG LIKE THAT!
HMM.
PLANET GIGANTIC
CROFTS
WRIGHT
ECKERT

IF SHE WAS HERE, SHE DIDN'T LEAVE ANY PAW PRINTS OR FUR BEHIND.
PLANET GIGANTIC
OOH.
GHOST DOG!
I'LL ASK AROUND. WHAT'S YOUR DOG'S NAME, KID?
OH!
LADY GAWRON.
HAH!
THAT'S GREAT.

THE SEARCH CONTINUES!
ONE TIME, LADY GOWRAN AND I WERE PLAYING.
AND SHE CHASED A RABBIT.
AND WE FOLLOWED IT DOWN A HOLE...
UH HUH.
LIKE A GAGILLION HOURS LATER...
AND THEN GOWRAN WAS LIKE SHABOOM!
SO GOWRAN TURNED HER PAWS INTO CHAIN-SAWS.
UH-HUH.
BUT KING NINJA WAS REALLY LOG-MAN.
No witnesses and no physical evidence.
IT'S LIKE THIS DOG DOESN'T EXIST ಠ_ಠ
Wait. Did he just say "chainsaw paws?"
HEY look at mike's comic!!! :O
WANT TO PLAY BAD COP?
ALWAYS!

HAVING FUN, MIKE?
BEST DAY EVER!
ICE CREAM AND COMICS AND YOU GUYS!
MOST KIDS WON'T HANG WITH ME FIVE MINUTES!
BUT WHAT ABOUT LADY GOWRAN?
I TOLD YOU! SHE'S FIGHTING KING NINJA!
WHICH GOWRAN ARE YOU TALKING ABOUT?
YOUR DOG?
OR THE BARBARIAN?
GASP!
LADY GOWRAN
KING NINJA STRIKES AGAIN!
JUST TELL US WHAT'S REALLY GOING ON, MIKE.
OR WE'RE DONE LISTENING.

MY FAMILY JUST MOVED HERE AND NO ONE WILL TELL STORIES WITH ME!
THEY JUST CALL ME A WEIRDO AND RUN AWAY.
THE BIG KIDS SAID YOU HELP PEOPLE.
SO I THOUGHT YOU'D LISTEN.
I THINK WE'VE BEEN SEARCHING FOR *THE WRONG THING.*
BUT I KNOW WHERE WE'LL FIND IT!
ICED DREAM

JUST FIND KIDS WHO LIKE PLAYING THE SAME WAY YOU DO!

HOW ABOUT THEM?
UMMM...

HEY!
YOU LIKE GOWRAN?
Y-YEAH.
DID Y'READ THE ONE WHERE SHE GETS MAD MOGUL TO SET HIS OWN HIDEOUT ON FIRE?
SQUEE!
GUESS THAT'S THE END OF THIS... PUPPY DOG TAIL!
YOU'RE PAW-FUL.
FIST-BUMP!
CASE CLOSED!

The Mason Middle Messenger

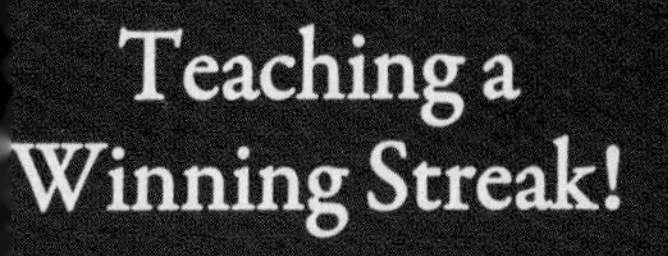

Teaching a Winning Streak!

Miss Maples claims sixth straight Teacher of the WeekAward!

Monica Potts shines in co-ed basketball semifinals!

Debate and Discourse

Can Dallas Cash give Mason their first win of the season?

Chapter Six:

"Mason Middle Messenger"

Written by Shawn Pryor

Artwork by Tressina Bowling

Lettering by Justin Birch

Pinup by Meg Daunting

Inez attempts to "Carrie" her team to victory in the Regional Wrestling Championship!

The Messenger Staff

Jackie Kirbee: E-I-C

Vanessa Bell: News Editor

Jerry Davis: Reporter

Sascha Patel: Reporter

Aliyah Aubreys: Photographer

Joe Davis: Layout Editor

“SQUAD!”

Theater
The Mason Middle School production of Alice in Wonderland was a smashing success, raising enough money to have a summer camp for our young thespians!
Special thanks to Trina Beeling for keeping the production together! :)

Go, Monica, Go!

Calvin with the defense!

Xaviera led the team in blocked shots and rebounds.

Co-Ed Basketball

Congrats to the Mason Middle School Co-Ed Basketball Team for winning three games in a row in the Inaugural Sectional Playoffs! Next stop, State Finals!

Harvey on the fast-break!

From Left to Right: (Front Row) Alison Beck, Harvey Jackson, Monica "Points" Potts, Trina Curry, Gabrielle Davis.
(Back Row) Coach Cambern, Calvin "Cooley" Lin, Xaviera "X-Factor" Reece, Taylor Thompson, Trey Tucker.

Mason's Inez Carrie (1st Place) with Barry Boggs (runner-up)

Inez Carrie continued her undefeated season at The Greater Mid-Conference Wrestling Regional Championship, defeating Carter Academy's Barry Boggs in the final round.

Will she break the Mason Middle School single season record for victories???

Debate Team/Chess Team

Dallas Cash leads a heated discourse for the Mason Middle School Debate Team.

However, Angela Bird had the last word and sealed a victory for Dilford Middle School.

Due to poor sportsmanship against Weaver Middle School, Khan Hudson has been suspended one game from the Mason Middle School Chess Team.

Who Will Be School President?
SCIENCE
VOTE ABBEY.
Abbey Edelman
Orlando Page
Billy Falls
Pacey Pacifica
Mabel Bay
Harold Welch
Your Vote Counts!

Science

The Mason Middle School Science Team (John Davies, Lori Preston, Marty Carty) attempted to build a robot for the local BotBattleWars Tournament, but were unsuccessful.

Don't give up, you'll get it right next time!

Teachers of the Week
Ms. Maples: Created a short film festival for the students to express themselves!
Mrs. Mills: Her students have perfect attendance!
Mr. Medluck: Completed the Tough & Rough Mudder Dash!
Mason Middle Munchies (aka Lunch)
Monday:
Power Pizza Slices, Crunchy Chips, Super Salad
Tuesday:
Hearty Hamburgers, Funky Fries, Party Pie
Wednesday:
Fish Fillet, Baked Broccoli Casserole
Thursday:
Cooley Club Sandwich, Perky Pickle Spears, Macho Macaroni & Cheese
Friday:
Walking Tacos, Casual Churros
GO LIONS!
RESPECT THE COOK

Pinup by Andy Jewett

Pinup by Jay Reed

1
Cash & Carrie Casefiles:
THE MYSTERY of the
MISSING MASCOT
Clue
Pinup by Kenny Keil